Far-Out Fir

Design by Michael Sund. Coordinated by Judy O. Productions, Inc.

MW01174433

Table of Contents:

Launch
take off from the ramp!

2

Ramp Up Your Ride!

Dude! One of the greatest things about finger bikes is you can turn almost anything into a cool park to show off all your tricks! You can jump your bike from almost anything—even the kitchen sink! You can even use this book. Create your very first ramp by taping the edge to a sturdy book—to create your very first ramp!

Trails
Performing stunts in the air over a series of dirt jumps

BUILD A PREMIUM PARK

You can build your own finger bike park by using boxes, tape, and your own creativity! Build ramps by taping sturdy pieces of cardboard to cereal boxes, packing boxes, shoe boxes—any size box you choose! Make the ramps as steep as you dare!

Your Own Set of Wheels!

Check out this awesome bike. This finger bike has working brakes, too. Push the button under the crossbar for the front brake. Push the seat down to activate the rear brake. You also have extra wheels, a bike stand, and a tool to help you adjust the pegs or change the wheels whenever you want.

Insert the rear spokes of bike to this bar

Push-Button Release

Bike Stand

Street
Performing stunts and tricks using obstacles/things found on the street.

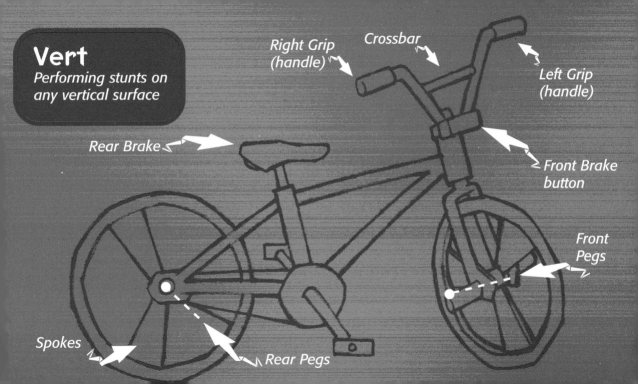

There are two basic starting positions:

Position 1

Put index finger on left grip, middle finger on right grip, thumb on left side of seat, and fourth and little finger on right side of seat. Reverse this, if you're a lefty.

Position 2

Put index finger under crossbar, middle and fourth finger on right of seat, and thumb on left side of seat. Again, lefties should reverse this.

Bar Dip

1 *Start in Position 1*

Flatland
Performing stunts on a smooth "flat" surface

2 *Launch.*

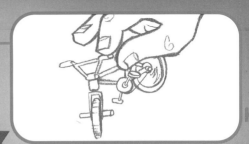
3 *While in air, take middle finger off grip, pull other grip towards seat with index finger.*

4 *Put middle finger back on grip and straighten bike out.*

5 *Land.*

Fakie Air

1 *Start in Position 1.*

Half-Pipe
ramp shaped like this:

Quarter-Pipe
ramp shaped like this:

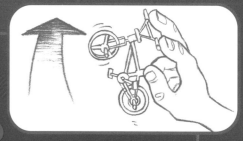

2 *Launch from ramp with front wheel straight up in the air and go as high (just straight up) as you can.*

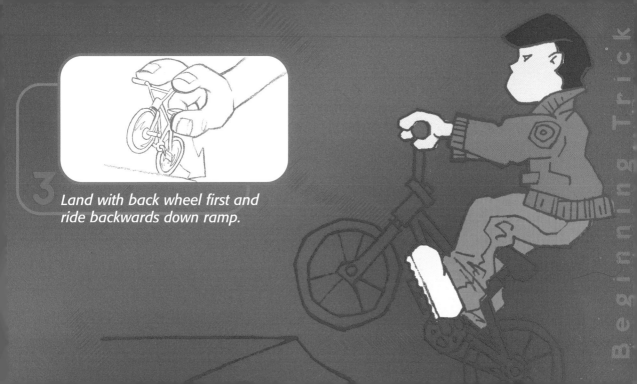

Land with back wheel first and ride backwards down ramp.

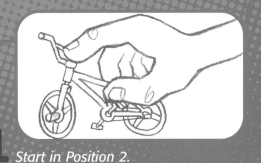

1 *Start in Position 2.*

2 *Launch!*

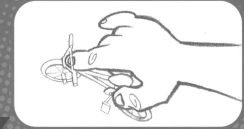

3 *When you are high in the air, make your bike straighten out so it's parallel to the ground.*

rail
short for guard or hand rail—any kind of railing

14

Tabletop

4 Land.

15

Beginning Tricks

Feeble Grind

1 Start in Position 2.

2 Hop bike into air and land on railing so back peg will touch the rail and front tires roll on rail in front.

3 Slide along rail.

transition
surface area of any ramps or jumps

4 *Toward the end of the rail pull up front wheel above the back wheel.*

5 *Slide bike off rail and land.*

Expert Trick

Launch from position 1.

While in the air take both fingers off handgrips and stretch them up in the air.

Return to position 1 while still in air.

18

No Hander

platform
top section of ramp—AKA 'deck'

Turndown

1 *Launch from position 2.*

lip
top edge of ramp

Twist bars back w/ middle finger.

Use middle finger and thumb to twist back of the bike down and to the side. Use index finger to turn bars around so they point down.

Level off and land!

You don't need a ramp for this one!

Tail Whip

Start in Position 2.

While rolling bike, press on front brake. As your back wheel raises, lift your middle finger and use your thumb to kick the back wheel up into the air so that it turns.

air
Getting the bike to jump as high as possible—that's "huge" or "sweet" air!

Let bike spin on the front wheel as many times as you can!

23

4 Land.

TRICK OR TREAT!

Create your own signature trick! You have the bike, the ramps, the know-how. Just use your imagination for the rest!